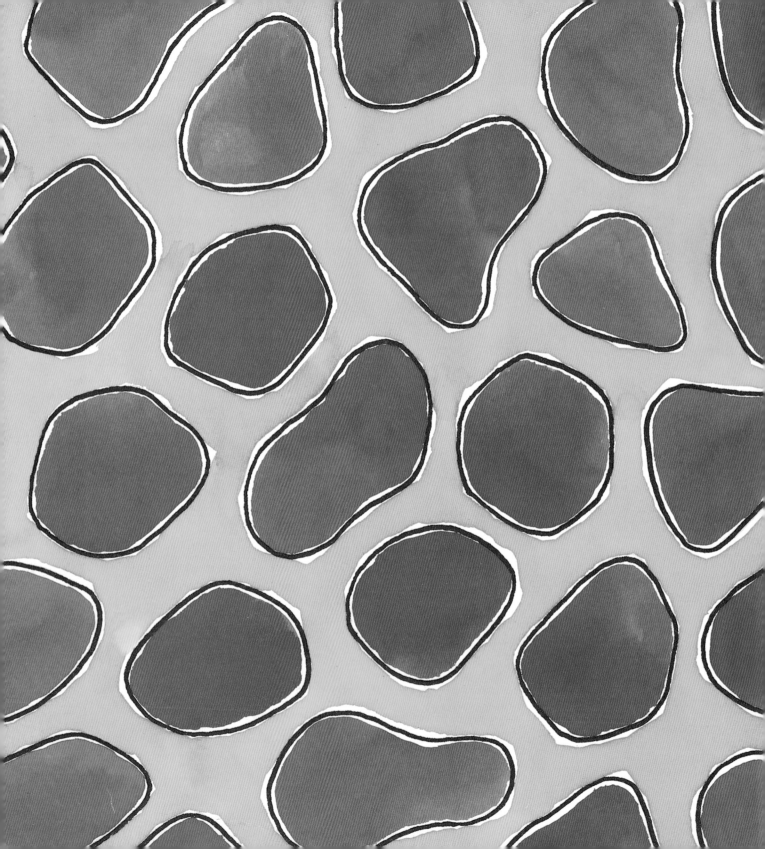

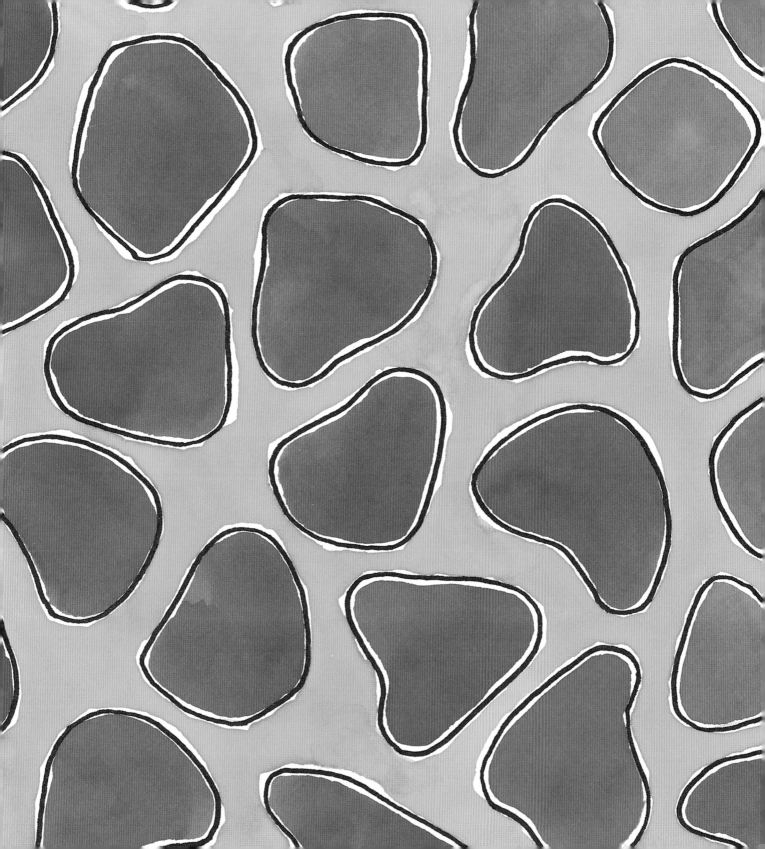

MYRIAD BOOKS LIMITED
35 Bishopsthorpe Road, London SE26 4PA

First published in Belgium and the Netherlands in 2004 by Clavis Uitgeverij, Hasselt-Amsterdam.

Text and illustrations copyright © 2004 Clavis Uitgeverij, Hasselt-Amsterdam.
All rights reserved.
www.clavisbooks.com

Judith Koppens has asserted her right under the Copyright, Designs and Patents Act 1998
to be identified as the author of this work.

ISBN 1 84746 071 2
EAN 978 184746 071 4

Printed in China

www.myriadbooks.com

Judith Koppens

Pig
and Giraffe

MYRIAD BOOKS LIMITED

Pig's best and biggest friend is Giraffe.

"Hey Giraffe," Pig says. "Can I give you a little kiss?"

"Of course," Giraffe says. "That would be great!"

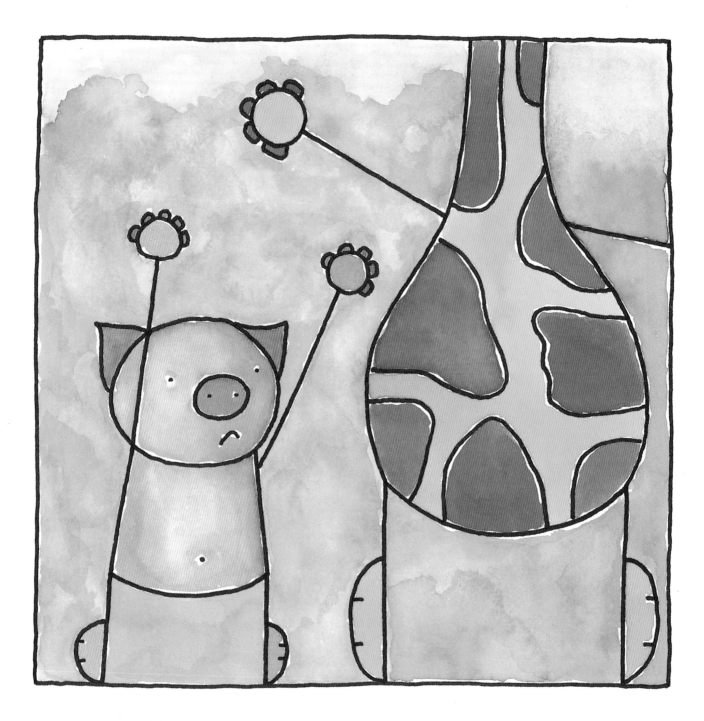

"But Giraffe," Pig says. "You are too big. I can't reach!"

"Not true, Pig," Giraffe says. "I am not too big.
You are too small!"

"You know what?" Pig says. "I'll dig a hole for you.
If you go and sit in it, then I can give you a kiss."

Pig digs and digs.
The hole becomes deeper and deeper.

But the hole is not deep enough.
Pig still can't give Giraffe a kiss.

"You know what?" Pig says. "I'll use a rope to swing.
Then I can give you a kiss."

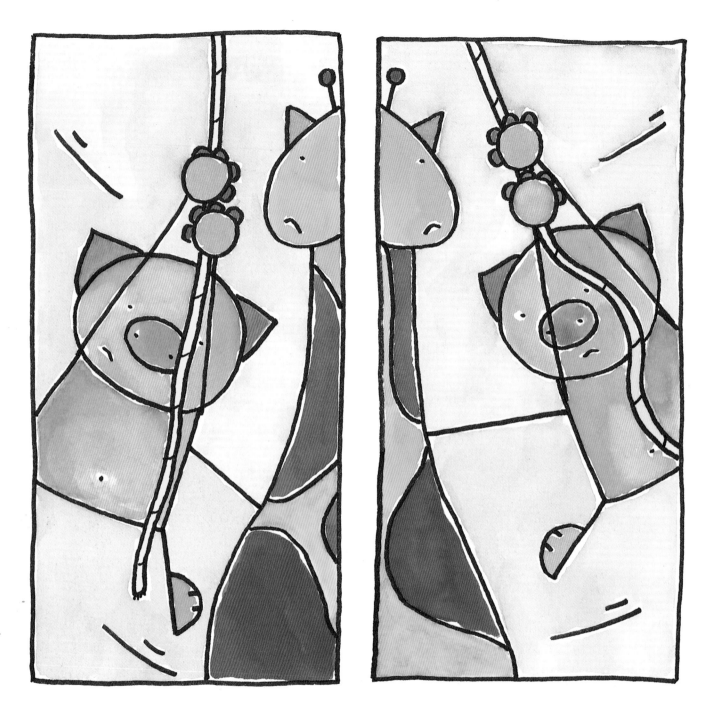

He sways and swings, as high up as he can.

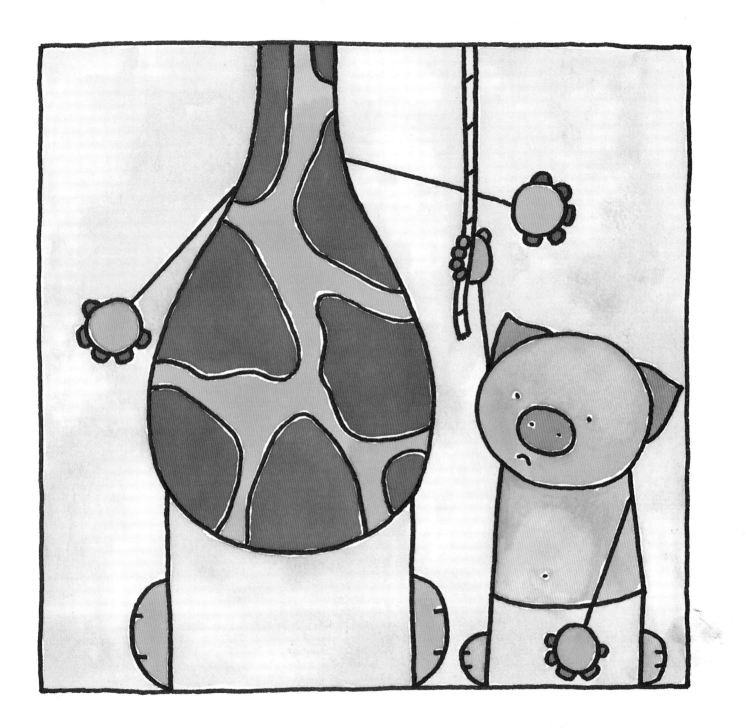

But each time he swings past Giraffe.
Pig still can't give Giraffe a kiss.

"You know what?" Pig says. "I'll run towards you
very fast and jump up very high.
Then surely I can give you a kiss."

Pig puts on fast sports shoes.
He runs to Giraffe as fast as he can.
Then he *jumps* up as high as he can.

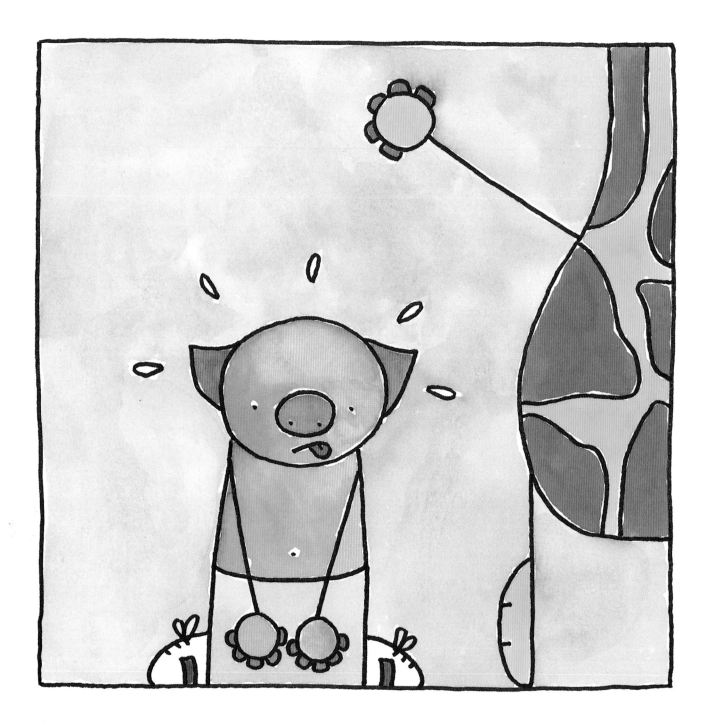

But Giraffe is too big.
Pig still can't give Giraffe a kiss.

"You know what?" Pig says. "I'll get a big ladder
and climb up. Then I can probably give you a kiss."

Pig slowly climbs up. But, oops, how high up that is!
It makes Pig shiver. And then...

"Help!" Pig calls out.
But it is too late already.

There Pig is, lying on the grass. His eyes are closed.

"Pig!" Giraffe calls out shocked.
"Does it hurt anywhere?"

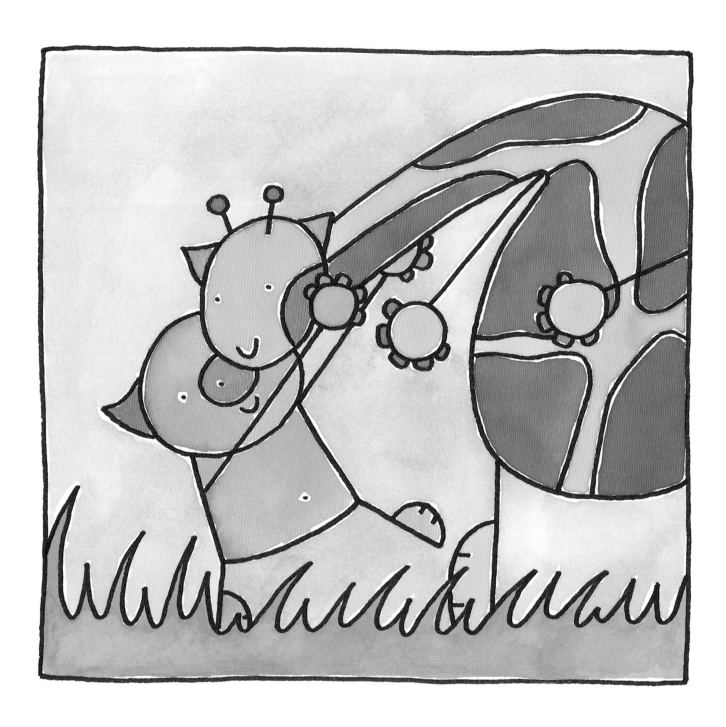

"Oh Giraffe," Pig says quietly.
"Finally I can give you a kiss."

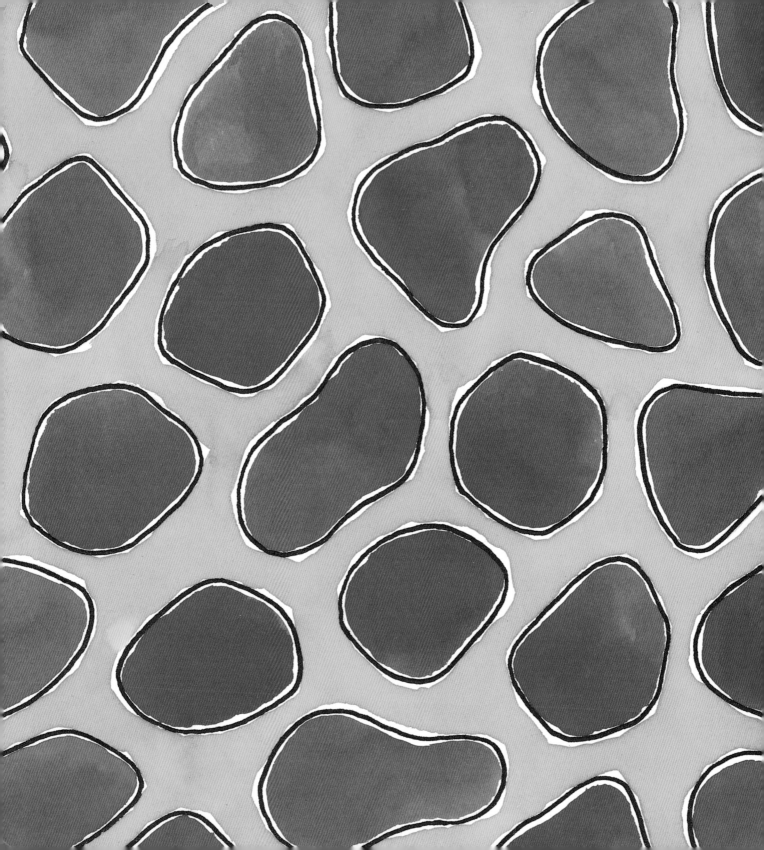

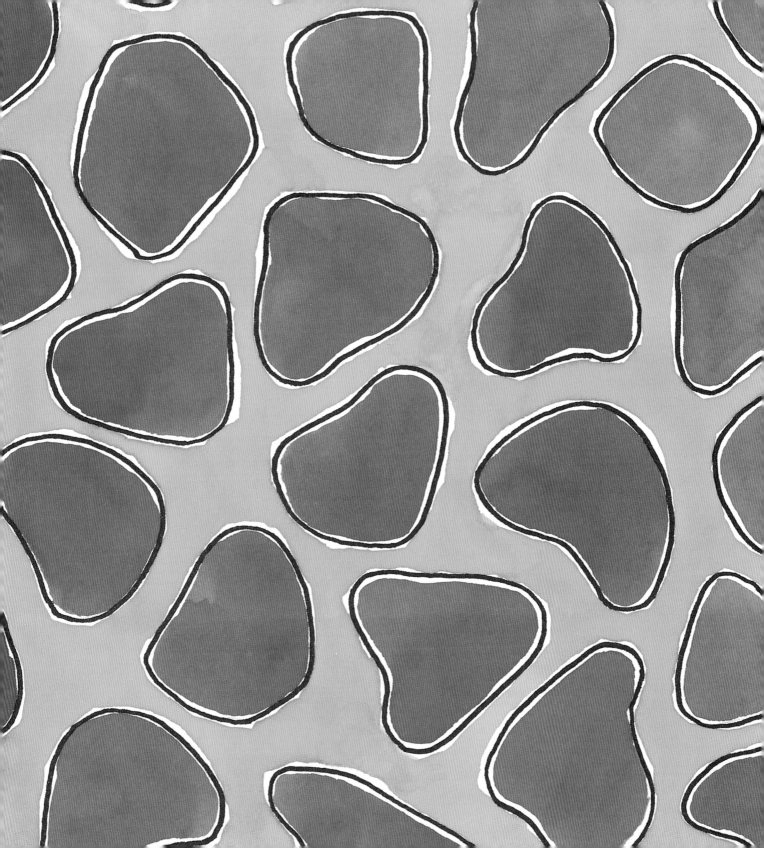